Olivia Beaumont

TALES

from the

Beautiful

MOUNTAIN

WRITTEN & ILLUSTRATED BY

OLIVIA BEAUMONT

First printing 2016

ISBN 978-0-692-4626-1-4

IngramSpark Publishing

Books may be purchased in quantity or special sales through the Ingram Content Group Inc.

Editor: Delisa Marchetti

Designer: Bevin Valentine Jalbert

Printed in the United States

Dedicated to my mother, who read to me at bedtime
(with all the character voices, too).

The Beautiful Mountain

At the top of the peak,
A noble heart you may seek,
A brave fox on the cliff,
You may spy.

Look way down below,
Where the river runs slow,
Three hedgehogs will sing,
By and by.

There deep dark within,
The light barely shines in,
A brown bear dreams,
of fish that fly.

The top is covered in snow,
And if you want to go,
Travel light like a bird,
To the Beautiful Mountain, so high.

The Tales

THE BEAR
AND THE DREAM

THE BEAR WENT TO HER DEN with a belly full of fish. She was ready for winter.

"Oh, it's time to hibernate again," she said. "The world will be warm and green again when I awaken. But, how lonely it is to be in my den all winter long," she sighed aloud. The bear lied down in the dark, warm den, and a deep sleep began to descend upon her.

She slept and slept, and twitched her nose. Her nose felt very itchy, and she noticed a miniature raccoon was crawling up her snout and tickling her whiskers! Then, a tiny elephant tugged the raccoon tail with its long nose. The den became

full of strange little creatures of all sizes and shapes. They pulled at tufts of the bear's fur while flying fish zipped through the air. All winter long, the little creatures kept the bear company.

One day, a trickle of melted snow reached her paw. She sighed and opened her drowsy eyes. Spring had arrived. The bear looked around the empty den and said, "What strange dreams I had!"

"Squeak!"

"What was that?" asked the bear. A mouse stretched sleepily in a ray of sunlight. She blinked up at the big bear and said, "I heard you say you were lonely and shared my dreams with you all winter long to keep you company."

So it was, that every year the bear and the mouse shared her warm den and filled it with strange and wonderful dreams until the spring had once again arrived.

The Cloud Palace

M EREK WAS A YOUNG MERLIN HAWK WITH STRONG dappled gray wings. He was fierce to look at, and he had a sharp beak and talons. He ruled the sky making sure that all the smaller jays, buntings, and mockingbirds stayed in their place. His strong wings helped him to fly higher than any other bird.

He flew so high one day that the clouds encircled him, and he could see only white mist. Around him were pillars of white that transformed into beautiful arches and columns. It was a grand white palace in the clouds. Merek felt powerful gusts of wind and saw a large pure white falcon flying next to him. She turned her dark eyes to look at him and she opened her beak to speak.

"I am called Reina, and I am queen of the Cloud Palace. You are welcome to come here anytime you like. You may go anywhere you please. I ask only that you never take anything from my palace back to earth or you will not be allowed to return here."

Reina flew away toward the center of the palace. Merek visited the beautiful palace every day. He would soar higher and higher until the mist thickened and the sparkling columns took form around him. He explored the halls and met other great birds who had all been welcomed to visit as often as they liked.

One day, Merek was in the Cloud Palace exploring a beautiful chamber filled with small puffy white clouds that dripped gently, forming delicate waterfalls into a larger basin. The little pond was so pure and clear. Merek saw something glinting in the pond. He pulled it out and saw that it was an armored breastplate. He put it around his neck and tried it on. It was pure silver with delicate chain mail that glistened as it hung off the neck plate. It was as light and weightless as his own feathers, but it was harder than steel.

Merek pranced proudly wearing the piece of armor. He thought to himself how impressed the little bluebirds and mockingbirds would be if they saw him now! He decided he would just go down to the earth quickly and come right back. So, downward he flew and as the mist became thinner and thinner, the breastplate got heavier and heavier. When he could see the earth again, the breastplate was so heavy that he plummeted faster and faster to the ground. He reached the earth, landing hard in a tree. He looked down and the armor was no longer silver, it had deepened into black metal and it was very heavy now. Merek found that he could not remove the armor from his neck. It weighed him down just enough that he could never fly quite as high to reach the misty clouds again. Merek tried many times to fly back to the Cloud Palace, but just as Reina had promised he was not allowed to return.

The breastplate had not lost all of its enchantment, though. There were times he thought he saw Reina flying high above him and the breastplate would glint silver just for a moment. Merek still ruled the little birds and the skies of earth and was famed for his tales of the Cloud Palace.

Southern Night

I T WAS A WARM SOUTHERN NIGHT IN JULY.
The air was soft, and the creatures around the swampland
moved slowly. The alligator had crept onto the bank and he was
tired of being lazy all day. He stamped his foot, Stomp! Stomp!
He liked the sound it made and thought to himself, "I have a beat
in my foot! Now, who has a tune?"

The alligator stompita-stompita-stomped! Just then, an
armadillo scurried by. The alligator's heavy tail crashed down and
knocked the armadillo over. It rolled into a ball and cried out,
"Please, don't eat me!"

"I will not eat you if you will provide the tune to the beat in my
feet," said the alligator, who stomped his feet wildly again.

The armadillo uncurled and said, "I can play you a tune on the
ukulele. First you will have to let me go home to collect it."

It was agreed, and soon the
armadillo returned with a tiny
ukulele and played a tune
as catchy as could
be. The alligator
stomped happily, and
their strange but merry little song
could be heard throughout the
whole swamp.

   Never had an alligator smiled so broad, as
he danced away that night. And, never had
the armadillo played better than he did that
night, when he played
for a price.

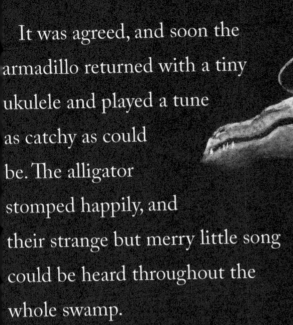

Olivia Beaumont

THE TALE OF ARCHER FOX

ARCHER FOX HAD JUST WITNESSED SOMETHING impossible. It had begun as a day like any other, when an owl had happened upon him in the woods.

"Hello, young fox," said the owl, who was pushing a cart loaded with goods for sale. "Would you like to buy something?"

"Good day," replied Archer, "What have you to sell?"

"I see that you carry an archer's bow," said the owl, "I have some very special arrows."

The owl produced three arrows and waved them under Archer's nose. The arrows did not look very special. They looked old and the shafts were bent.

"No, I do not want those," said Archer.

"Oh yes, you do. Let me tell you how special they are. If you shoot one of these arrows at a living thing, it will no longer remain alive. However, if you shoot one of these arrows at a non-living thing, it will come to life for a day."

"Hah!" laughed Archer, "You probably just pulled those old bent arrows out of a tree. How do I know that they will do what you say?"

The old owl squinted his giant golden eyes and replied, "If you do not believe me, then you may shoot one of the arrows at that stone, there. You will see for yourself."

Archer put the arrow to his bow and aimed. He released the bow and the arrow shot through the air. To Archer's surprise, the arrow pierced the stone, rather than bouncing off. The stone parted in the middle and formed an opening that looked like a red mouth with ugly gray teeth. Then two eyes opened. They were black and shiny as pebbles. Blinking, the stone creature tottered forward. Archer was stunned. Shivers ran down his spine to his tail. The stone had come to life. The little stone wandered off into the woods, perhaps looking for others like itself.

Archer paid for the arrows, and the owl bumbled away down the path with his cart of strange goods. Archer had two enchanted arrows remaining. How would he use them?

Archer climbed a tall tree and looked in every direction. He put one arrow to the bow and scanned the horizon looking for a mark. Some twigs cracked under Archer's foothold in the tree. Just then a family of crows burst loudly out of their nest. They startled Archer so much that he let go of the bow string. The enchanted arrow catapulted wildly through the air. Then, it spiraled downward, but Archer could not tell where it would land. Finally, the arrow touched the ground, settling its sharp point into a slope of dirt.

To his dismay, Archer heard a low rumble and the trees began to sway. The arrow had landed in the dirt, but the dirt belonged to the slope of a very, very tall mountain. The mountain was coming to life. Archer watched in disbelief as the mountain opened two wide eyes that sparkled like diamond mines in the cliff side and a large mouth, out of which poured a massive waterfall. Trees on the surface of the mountain were coming uprooted and creating rockslides that

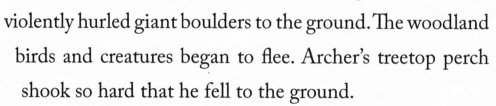 violently hurled giant boulders to the ground. The woodland birds and creatures began to flee. Archer's treetop perch shook so hard that he fell to the ground.

Archer picked himself up and ran in fear. He once again saw the small stone creature tottering away yelping in alarm. A thought occurred to Archer. He stopped running away, and turned left toward a valley. He now had an unobstructed view of the living mountain. Archer Fox was a brave soul, but even he felt frightened as he beheld the Mountain Giant heaving its mass skyward and attempting to stand on its own two feet. It was so tall that its head was above the clouds. The Mountain Giant bent his head low and those beautiful, strange, sparkling eyes peered down at Archer through the misty clouds.

"You really are something to behold," shouted Archer to the Mountain Giant, "but I am afraid you are too grand for our little world. You will be much happier when you are sleeping again."

With that, Archer took aim and shot the last arrow. It pierced the Mountain Giant's foot. Down came the mass of rock and earth, falling from the sky. With a resounding thud, the Mountain Giant was laid on the earth, asleep once more. Archer sighed in relief. To this day, the mountain has the faint outline of a giant man, and the peak with two caves and a waterfall is called Giant's Head Peak.

LEVERETTE
AND THE GARDEN

Leverette's long rabbit ears trailed behind him as he hopped down into his rabbit hole carrying several heads of lettuce. He made five more trips to the garden and back carrying loads of carrots, parsnips, and lettuces. He had worked hard on his vegetable garden, and now he was yielding his first big crop. He planned to harvest as much as he could and then have his friends over for a banquet.

Leverette looked contentedly at the heap of bright vegetables. He was going to throw such a party!

"I will just test this lettuce for crispness," he thought to himself, and he munched the lettuce right down to the core. It was so good, he ate three more.

"While I am at it, I may as well test out the parsnips and the carrots," thought Leverette. He ate more of the sweet, crisp carrots than he could count. Then he ate a dozen parsnips and a few more lettuces for good measure.

"Delicious!" he exclaimed, wiping his whiskers with a long ear, "My friends will enjoy the feast very much." But he did not stop eating. The more he ate, the more he praised his vegetable crop, and the more he wanted to taste it again. Finally, Leverette had grown very sleepy. He stretched his arms and yawned. His stomach bulged out of his red coat and his shirt buttons strained against the pressure. He took off his coat and lied down, falling asleep. He dreamed of the beautiful vegetable banquet he would share with his friends.

When he woke, he thought, "I feel like a tasty carrot would be just the thing!" He went to look at his heap of vegetables, but to his surprise there was not much left. Only a few heads of lettuce and a single parsnip lay there.

"Thief!" yelped Leverette.

As he stood in astonishment, his bulging stomach gurgled loudly, and he remembered that he was the thief who had greedily eaten all of the vegetables. So, Leverette invited his good friend Pip over. Together they shared the last of the lettuce. Leverette told him the story of his daylight thief, and they laughed and cried over the banquet Leverette had eaten all by himself.

ESSENTIAL FINERY

WINTA WAS A PLAINS ZEBRA, BUT SHE WAS BY NO MEANS PLAIN. She wore her stripes boldly, elegant black contour lines tapering at her delicate nose. When the herd of zebras ran in startled frenzy from danger, Winta made a point to trot gracefully around the mud puddles not wanting to dirty her lustrous tail. As the herd grazed, Winta would pause around colorful patches of wildflowers and weave them into her mane. She often cast her eyes toward the sky and fancied she saw images in the fluffy savannah clouds. The others reminded her that a zebra should keep her mind on only two things: staying close to the herd, and away from danger. However, Winta felt a passionate embrace of the beauty around her, a desire to embellish her world, and clearly, she had a sense of fashion.

One day, the herd was on the move, following the river as it twisted and wound over the flat land. An abandoned human encampment lay alongside a dry bank. A dark ashen mark had scorched the ground where a fire had burned a few nights ago. The zebra herd plodded on, a few nuzzling around the fire to

detect food traces. Winta poked her nose inside a large canvas bag. She pulled out an object. It was a chess board. Small ivory playing pieces rolled out on the ground beside it. She next pulled out a hat box with a bonnet inside, a few belts, a pipe, a pair of red spectacles, a tangle of many colored ribbons, and lastly a swatch of golden fabric. She laid them all out on the ground in front of her. The fabric looked to be a ladies' bodice. It was richly decorated with myriads of hand-embroidered blossoms and curling vines delicately stitched in gold, scarlet, and emerald thread. The whole garment shimmered in the sunlight, reflecting off tiny crystals threaded onto the fabric.

Winta pushed her nose into the opening of the bodice, slipping it over her head, and shaking it gently into place on her neck. She turned her head from side to side casting her eyes upon the finery. Other zebras had noticed her, and stood in a circle around her. A female zebra snorted.

"You cannot wear patterns with stripes," she announced.

Winta bowed her head, clasped the bonnet between her teeth and placed it on the female zebra's head.

"You," pronounced Winta, "look marvelous. See how it keeps the sun off your ears?"

The bonneted zebra glared at Winta and went to the river crouching to see her reflection.

"I do look marvelous!" she cried, batting her dark lashes, "Let me try the spectacles!"

Winta removed the bonnet and placed the spectacles on her nose.

"So distinguished," she crooned.

The other zebras began tying the belts and ribbons on their necks, manes, and tails. A few in the herd had little fashion sense at all and instead put the abandoned cooking pots on their heads. Winta quickly helped them to find something less utilitarian and more colorful. The whole herd looked splendid. Packs of lions and hyenas would watch, mouth agape, as this colorful society passed them by. No beast would dare to take a bite out of a lady like Winta and her finery.

The Historian
and the Princess

THERE WAS A HISTORIAN WHO BECAME WELL KNOWN IN his village for his encyclopedic knowledge of everything. He was handsome enough, though he was a hairy boar, but no one minded much about that because he was polite and he was so smart. The villagers would ask him questions just to test him, but he always gave an accurate answer. One day, the king learned about the historian and invited him to come show his unique skills at the palace. The king was so impressed with the vast knowledge of the historian that he invited him to become a council member of his royal court. He dressed him in fine clothes and gave him a room in the castle and a library where he could write down in books everything he knew.

The historian had grown used to always being right. He was proud of his talent for cataloging and remembering the history

of everything. One day the king asked him something that he did not know. He stood there, the sweat beading up on his brow, and then nervously made something up. The answer pleased the king, and no one knew the historian had lied because he was never wrong about anything.

However, the king's daughter noticed his nervousness. She wrote an anonymous note and left it in his library. When the historian found the note his pig nose turned a shade of pink.

The note read, *I know what you did. Meet me in the garden near the fountain, tonight.*

The historian felt very guilty as he waited near the fountain that night. A dark shrouded figure approached him. He could not see the face of the princess under the veil.

The princess approached him and said, "I came to ask you a very important question. You are the historian, and you have a reputation for being right all the time. This means you are truthful all the time. Did you speak truthfully today?"

The historian shook his head sadly, "No. I lied to the king. It's never happened before, and I just became nervous. Please, believe me, I will tell the king what I have done. People are wrong about me, I'm not always right. After all, I'm only a humble pig from the village."

The princess removed her veil and smiled, "No, indeed. No one is always right. Besides, no one likes a person who insists on being right all the time! But what you are, historian, is always truthful. That is a rare quality, and the palace is just where you belong with my father and perhaps with me."

The historian returned to his post, a humbled pig, but he knew the princess was right. The historian never lied again and grew to have more than mere knowledge, but wisdom, too. One year later, when it was time for the princess to take her place as ruler and find a husband she married the handsome and wise historian.

THE HOGGENS BROTHERS

HEDGY, PRICK, AND POKE WERE A TRIO OF TINY musicians. Very tiny. In fact, they were hedgehogs. Yet, they had grown tired of playing music for their hedge-families who cared more for digging and grubs than they did music. So the Hoggens brothers decided they would go into town and strike up a concert for the people who lived there.

While on their journey, the sound of a fiddle lulled over the hills and caught their ears. They followed it and they met a boy who was playing a fiddle. The three brothers started to play along on the violin, bass, and pipe. The boy was amazed. He gathered up the three hedgehogs without so much as an introduction and ran all the way back to town.

"Look, Mother! These hedgehogs were playing a song on the

hill," said the boy.

But, in his hurry, the boy had dropped the tiny musical instruments up on the hill. His mother looked at the three creatures, hushed the boy, and told him to wash up for dinner. After dinner, he took them out again and showed his father.

"Father, these hedgehogs played music!"

His father was reading and hushed the boy again. The house was quiet, so the boy set the hedgehogs on a chair in his bedroom. He set his own fiddle down on the chair, and right away the hedgehogs went to work, plucking out a tune, all three of them bouncing on the strings.

The next day, the boy took the hedgehogs back to the hill and found their tiny instruments. The hedgehogs decided that they would stay in the woods from now on. Day after day, they would meet the boy on top of the hill and teach him their songs. They took great pleasure in this, and when the boy grew up he was a well known musician noteworthy for the beautiful and unusual songs he played.

LEANDER
AND THE LOST RING

A KING HAD LOST A RUBY RING, AND HE HAD DECLARED that whoever found the ring and returned it would receive a reward. He did not say what kind of reward it would be, but the whole kingdom searched day and night for the priceless ring.

Leander, the tiger, was the Falcon Master at the castle. There was one falcon that belonged to Leander alone, and he would spend much time in the hills around the castle practicing the art of falconry with her. She was a beautiful and swift bird, and he had given her the name, Calixte, meaning "most beautiful".

One day Calixte brought down a small sparrow. Leander retrieved the catch. As Calixte gently unfurled her claws he noticed a red gleam of light around the sparrow's leg. It was the ruby ring, lost by the king.

"Look, Calixte," said Leander, "now we will have the riches of a king when we return this ring to him.

The little sparrow cried out, "No! You will not prosper if you do this thing! Let me ask you, what reward does the King offer?"

"He did not say more than that," replied Leander. "Certainly a king's reward will be lavish."

"You are wrong again," replied the sparrow, "the king is a suspicious man. He believes that when the ring is found the thief will be found. His reward will be to banish that man from the kingdom!"

"Then how did you get the ring?" asked Calixte.

"I know who the real thief is," admitted the sparrow. "It was the king's advisor who put this ring on my foot. He knew the king suspected a thief."

Leander wondered aloud, "The royal advisor? Everyone knows what a harsh and hateful man he is. He is the very reason the King has become so suspicious. The kingdom would be better off without him. I know what we must do, Calixte!"

While the king and the advisor were dining, Calixte and the sparrow entered from a high window. The sparrow flew

down, knocking a lamp stand over and while both of the men were distracted, Calixte flew silently above them low enough to drop the ring into the evil advisor's pocket. Then Leander entered and requested audience with the king.

Leander said, "Thank you, your Highness. I would like to know what you would do if a subject of your kingdom could tell you who stole your ruby ring?"

The king replied, "I suspected it was stolen. If that was the case I would have the thief banished, and the one who told me would be made a high officer of my court."

Leander pointed at the advisor and said, "It was him."

The advisor was immediately searched, and the ruby ring was found right where Calixte had carefully dropped it. He was banished, and the king chose Leander to be the new advisor in his place. Under the rule of the king and his new good advisor the kingdom prospered for many years.

Jessamine and the Blue Footprints

Mr. Augustus Spebbington lived with his wife, Bernice, and two children, Theodore and Jessamine, in the hollow of a magnolia tree. They were happy and nobody ever bothered them. Perhaps it was due to the fact that they were a family of skunks, or it may have been that Mr. Spebbington simply preferred the peace and quiet. Thus, it was one night that a problem arose for Mr. Spebbington that he never expected. Some creature had taken to making the most horrible noises outside Mr. Spebbington's window at night. Poor Mr. Spebbington had almost no sleep for three nights.

On the fourth night, Mr. Spebbington had gone to bed and was once again rudely awoken by the noise. It sounded as if some awful monster was trying to sing a raucous tune. He simply could stand no more! He grabbed a handful of walnuts and hurled them out the window, one at a time, in the direction of the noise. He could see nothing in the dark, but he heard, "Ow! Ow! Yeeeoouch!" and after that the noise stopped.

The next morning Mr. Spebbington was sitting at breakfast with his wife and daughter, telling them how he had thrown walnuts at the rude noise in the night.

He asked little Jessamine, "Where is your brother?"

Jessamine replied, "He said he had a headache. I'll go upstairs and check on him."

Jessamine went to the bedroom door and called out to her brother. She heard a muffled groan, and he opened the door. Theodore was holding his head, but she noticed he also had an ugly knot on his neck and his paw, too.

"Would you like some breakfast? I can bring it upstairs for you."

"Yes." groaned Theodore.

Jessamine went back to the table and asked her mother for some toast and blueberry jam, then she went back upstairs to her brother's bedroom.

That night Jessamine went to bed, but she deliberately stayed awake until the house was quiet. She peeked out of her bedroom door. There! Theodore's bedroom door was open. Blue footprints trailed down the stairs. Earlier that day she had

rubbed blueberry jam on the bottom of his slippers while he was eating toast. She crept down the stairs following the footprints. They led out the front door just as she had suspected. Then she saw her brother. Theodore was behaving very strangely. He seemed to be sleepwalking, stumbling around in the dark in his night shirt and bedroom slippers. All the frogs and night creatures had gathered round and were laughing heartily at sleepy little Theodore. Theodore bumped into a toad and mumbled half coherently, "Well that's the ugliest dragon I've ever seen."

To this, the frogs laughed even harder, stamping their feet, and the owls fell out of the trees hooting at the ensuing hilarity. Jessamine scolded the frogs for laughing at her unaware little brother. She took Theodore's paw and gently led him back to the house.

The next morning the Spebbington family had a laugh, too, when Jessamine explained what had caused the awful noises outside her father's window. Theodore decided he would rather lock his bedroom door at night, and they lived peacefully ever after.

Cowardly Basil

Young Basil was about as un-curious as a little elephant could be. Everything frightened him. His father was a portrait painter, and had asked Basil to go to the village to buy new paint brushes and a tin of ochre.

Basil cried, "Father, I cannot go to the village. What if, along the way, stinging ants crawl into my trunk and bite me? What if a wasp buzzes in my ear and stings me? What if a raven lands on me and pulls my hair?"

His father shook his head and resolved to do something to help his son become more courageous. He patted his trembling little boy on the head and went back to the art studio. Basil's father stayed in there for a long time and only came out for dinner. Afterwards, he told little Basil to come into the studio.

There, his father showed him a painting on the easel. The portrait was of a young elephant in a blue coat. It looked just like little Basil, right down to the crop of fuzz atop his head, but there was a striking difference. In the portrait, Basil stood looking confident and polished.

"This is a portrait of you, my son," said Basil's father. "Whenever you look at this painting you will be filled with courage and you won't be afraid anymore. As

long as you have the painting you won't have to be afraid of ants or wasps or ravens, anymore."

As Basil gazed at the handsome portrait his stature straightened and he ruffled his ears happily. He was proud of the painting and thought that he even looked heroic. Just as promised, he was no longer afraid of ants, wasps, ravens, or anything else, for as long as he had the painting.

Olivia Beaumont

Josephine
and the
Impossible Radish

Josephine's favorite pasttime was reading in the library. She could sit cozied up for hours in the wood-paneled room which smelled of leather and dust. She imagined the library was her forest, and it was here that she would have all of her adventures. One day she picked up a book that had fallen off the shelf and noticed a green leaf shoot coming out of the pages. She pulled on it and out rolled a red radish. The book did not have any title on the leather dust jacket, so Josephine opened the cover. There was a handwritten inscription on the inside. It read: *1. Check for seeds. 2. Plant sparingly.*

"How odd," she thought. Shaking the book, four tiny seeds fell from the pocket of the dust jacket into her hand. She decided that she would plant a single seed in a pot and set it near the window.

Josephine took the book to bed that night, but the text was written in a language she could not read. The next morning she went to the library to see if

the tiny seed had sprouted. It had! A giant red radish had burst the pot and had grown into the floor of the library. A large sprout of greens and half of a giant radish were visible above the ground.

Josephine wondered what to do with a radish as big as she was. She frantically looked for a book on gardening. She found it and turned to the section on harvesting root vegetables. It said: *Harvesting a radish is fairly easy. To remove it from the ground, grab the radish at the base of its greens and pull straight up.*

Josephine grasped the base of the greens and pulled. The radish popped out easily, as promised. Josephine smiled to herself, comforted by the reliability of her books. Then she noticed the deep hole in the library floor. She kneeled down to examine it. It was very deep, and the harder she peered into it, the deeper it seemed to become. Before she could catch herself, she fell into the hole.

Her dress had gotten dirty in the fall, but she was fine. She could have easily climbed back out, but she noticed there were tunnels branching off the main hole and she wanted to explore first. She followed a tunnel and when it came to the end she opened a door and peered inside. What she saw was impossible! It looked like a scene out of a story she had read last week. The heroine from the story stood before a dragon, bravely holding a sword. Josphine closed the door, chose another passage, and opened another door. Here she saw two dogs in a rowboat trying to reel in a monster fish. She had read that story a few weeks ago. At the end of each passage was a door, and behind the door was a glorious world of fiction.

Josephine realized the enchantment of the radish seeds. She found her way back to the original hole and climbed up into her familiar library. The large red radish was withering away rapidly. No telling how long it would last. Decisively, she took the leather book with the three remaining seeds and put it carefully into a satchel, tying it around her waist. Ready to go, Josephine leapt back into the hole with the sparkle of adventure in her eyes.

CPSIA information can be obtained
at www.ICGtesting.com
Printed in the USA
LVOW05*0711081216
516366LV00012B/47/P